A

After the Buffalo Jump

A Story of the Blackfoot Nation

by Godwin Chu

Don Johnston Incorporated
Volo, Illinois

Edited by:
Jerry Stemach, MS, CCC-SLP
Speech/Language Pathologist, Director of Content Development, Start-to-Finish ™ Books

Gail Portnuff Venable, MS, CCC-SLP
Speech/Language Pathologist, San Francisco, California

Dorothy Tyack, MA
Learning Disabilities Specialist, San Francisco, California

Consultant: Ted S. Hasselbring, PhD
William T. Brian Professor of Special Education Technology, University of Kentucky

Copy Editor: Susan Kedzior

Cover Design and Illustrations: Susan Baptist and Jeff Ham

Interior Illustrations and Photographs: Jeff Ham, Susan Baptist, Glenbow Archives, Calgary, Canada; National Archives, Rocky Mountain Region

Read by: Jim DeNomie

Audio Producer: Mark Blottner

Sound Engineer: Tom Krol, *TK Audio Studios*

Copyright © 2001 Start-to-Finish™ Publishing. All rights reserved.

The Don Johnston logo and Start-to-Finish™ are trademarks of Don Johnston Incorporated. All rights reserved.

Published by:

Don Johnston Incorporated
26799 West Commerce Drive
Volo, IL 60073
800.999.4660 USA Canada
800.889.5242 Tech Support
www.donjohnston.com

Printed in the U.S.A. No part of this publication may be reproduced, stored in a retrieval system or transmitted in any form or by any means electronic, mechanical photocopying recording, or otherwise.

International Standard Book Number
ISBN 1-58702-673-2

Contents

Chapter 1
In the Beginning 5

Chapter 2
The Meaning of Names 18

Chapter 3
Buffalo Days 28

Chapter 4
The Buffalo Jump 36

Chapter 5
Preparing for Winter 50

Chapter 6
The Sun Dance 60

Chapter 7
The White People Come 70

Chapter 8
Lame Bull's Treaty 80

Chapter 9
Death in Montana 90

Chapter 10
Treaty Number 7 100

Bibliography 107

A Note from the Start-to-Finish™ Editors

About the Reader

Jim DeNomie is a member of the Bad River Band of Chippewa Indians of Lake Superior in Wisconsin. He visits schools to give talks about Native American culture and about the Native Americans who live near the Western Great Lakes. Jim is the Host and Co-Producer of a radio program about Native Americans called *Voices from the Circle*. This program is available on the internet at www.airos.org, and on the American Indian Radio On Satellite (AIROS) network. Jim works on social justice issues for Native Americans and other minority groups.

Chapter 1

In the Beginning

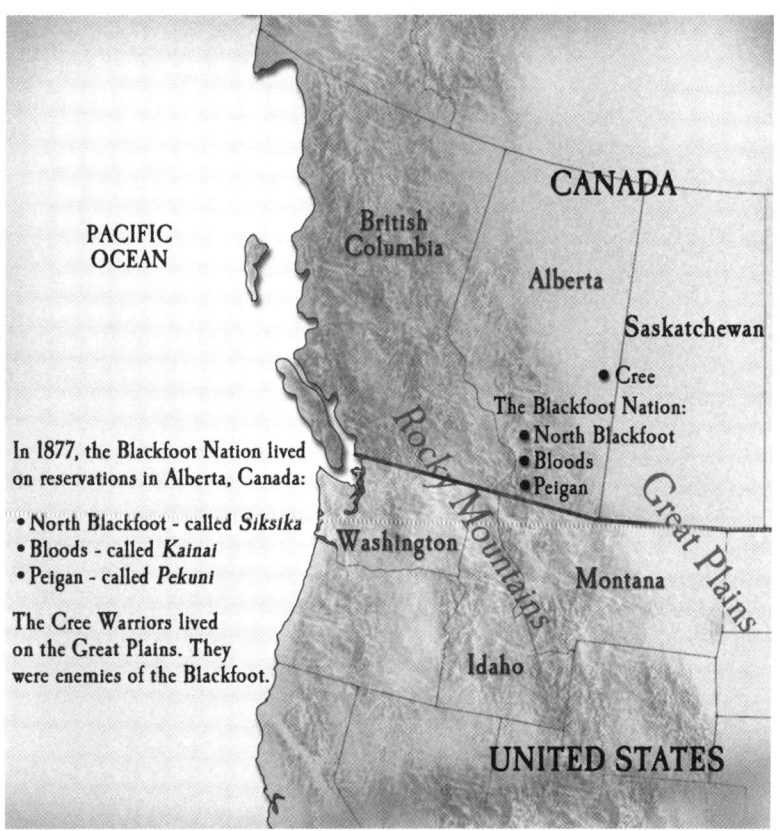

In 1877, the Blackfoot Nation lived on reservations in Alberta, Canada:

- North Blackfoot - called *Siksika*
- Bloods - called *Kainai*
- Peigan - called *Pekuni*

The Cree Warriors lived on the Great Plains. They were enemies of the Blackfoot.

The Blackfoot Nation:
- North Blackfoot
- Bloods
- Peigan

The Blackfoot Indians live on the grassy plains of North America. When we say "Blackfoot," we are really talking about three different tribes of people.

In English, we call one of the tribes the North Blackfoot. These people call themselves *Siksika* in the Blackfoot language.

We call another one of the Blackfoot tribes the Bloods. The Bloods call themselves *Kainai* in the Blackfoot language.

We call the third Blackfoot tribe Peigan. The Peigan people call themselves *Pekuni* in the Blackfoot language.

For hundreds of years before the white man came, the three different Blackfoot tribes lived near one another and shared the same language and the same way of life. They even helped each other fight wars against their enemies.

The Blackfoot were nomads. Nomads are people who move from place to place all year long.

A Step into History

The Blackfoot depended on buffalo for their food, clothing and tools, so they followed the great herds of buffalo as they moved across the plains. A few hundred years ago, there were millions of buffalo on the grassy plains of North America.

Where did the buffalo come from? Where did the Blackfoot people come from?

Blackfoot people like Charlie Panther Bone or Bernard Big Snake or Donald Shot Both Sides would tell a special Blackfoot story about how the world was made. It is called a creation story. This is how the story goes.

In the beginning, the world was all water. It was one big ocean with no land.

The creator of the world was Napi. In English, we call him "Old Man."

Chapter 1   After the Buffalo Jump   **11**
A Story of the Blackfoot Nation

Glenbow Archives, Calgary, Canada (NB-21-13)

In those days, Old Man did not have any other people to keep him company. He lived with some of the animals.

One day, Old Man asked the animals, "What's at the bottom of the ocean?" So one by one, Duck, then Otter, then Badger dived down into the water. But none of them could hold their breath long enough to reach the bottom of the ocean.

So Old Man sent Muskrat into the water. Muskrat stayed down for so long that Old Man was afraid he had drowned.

But after a long time, Muskrat came back to the top. He was holding a little ball of mud between his paws.

Old Man smiled at Muskrat. Then Old Man took some of the mud and breathed on it. The mud began to grow. It kept growing until it became the earth. Now there were mountains and valleys and grassy plains.

Old Man took more of the mud and made a woman to keep him company. He called her "Old Woman." Then Old Man and Old Woman made more people.

As each year passed, there were more and more people. Old Man and Old Woman had to decide how all of these people should live.

Old Man said to Old Woman, "Since I made you, *I* should have the first word about how people should live."

"I agree," Old Woman replied. "But if you have the first word, then I shall have the last word."

At first, the people were cold and hungry, so Old Man and Old Woman showed them how to eat plants.

Old Man and Old Woman taught the people how to make tools and how to catch animals for food. But after a while, there were just too many people to feed.

Old Woman said to Old Man, "There will never be enough plants and animals to feed all these people. Maybe people should not live forever. If people are hungry, they will fight with each other."

At first, Old Man did not agree with her. But Old Woman had the last word. "People should die when they get old," she said.

"That way, new people can have a chance to live," continued Old Woman. "People will care about each other more if they know that they are going to die."

So, people lived and died. The people made families, and the families lived together in groups. They worked together and helped each other. They moved across the earth looking for food. They played and hunted when the weather was warm, and they huddled together when the weather was cold. Some of the people became Blackfoot.

Chapter 1 — After the Buffalo Jump
A Story of the Blackfoot Nation

The Blackfoot lived on the Great Plains. Today, that part of the Great Plains is called Montana in the United States and Alberta in Canada. But in 1843, when this story begins, it was just the land that Old Man had made for his people. The Blackfoot lived free on the Great Plains. And the plains were filled with buffalo.

Chapter 2

The Meaning of Names

Chapter 2 — After the Buffalo Jump
A Story of the Blackfoot Nation

Good Eagle and Little Leaf were Blackfoot, and they were husband and wife. Little Leaf had given birth to twins, a boy and a girl.

Little Leaf sat outside her teepee, and held her babies close to her in the warm sunshine. Nearby, a small boy named Buffalo Tail poked at some rocks with a stick. Buffalo Tail was the son of a Blackfoot warrior named Running Wolf.

Good Eagle and Running Wolf were away from camp looking for buffalo. They had been gone for three days.

It was early springtime, and the snow was beginning to melt. The tribe had just moved from its winter camp in the woods to the grassy, open plains. Little Leaf hoped that Good Eagle and Running Wolf would return soon.

Suddenly Buffalo Tail pointed with his stick. "Father," he said out loud.

Little Leaf looked into the sun. She could see Running Wolf and her husband riding toward the camp. She watched the men tie up their horses, and wave at her and the children.

Little Leaf and Good Eagle were happy to see each other again.

"Did you find the buffalo?" Little Leaf asked her husband.

"No, but it is still early," Good Eagle answered. "I'm sure we will find them soon."

"Yes, I'm sure you will," Little Leaf agreed. She knew that they *had* to find the buffalo soon or their people would starve, but she kept her fears to herself.

Good Eagle took his two children in his arms and showed them to his friend, Running Wolf.

"Your children are beautiful," Running Wolf said. "Now it is time to give them names."

"Yes, it is time," Good Eagle said. "Running Wolf, it would be a great honor to us if you would choose names for them."

"I would be happy to give names to your children," Running Wolf replied.

Blackfoot Indians take their names seriously. Children are given their names by an important person in the tribe, like a chief or a warrior. The name often tells something about the life of the important person. So, a Blackfoot name can make you think about two people. First, you think about the person who *has* the name. Second, you think about the person who *gave* the name.

Two years earlier, Good Eagle had given the name of Buffalo Tail to Running Wolf's son.

24 A Step into History

Now it was time for Running Wolf to do the same for the children of his friend.

After the evening meal, they all went inside the teepee. They sat in a circle around a fire. Good Eagle added more dried buffalo droppings to the fire, and Running Wolf began to tell a story.

"One day when I was a young warrior, I was returning from a battle against our enemy, the Cree," explained Running Wolf. "There were eight Cree warriors chasing me. They had killed all of the other Blackfoot warriors, so I was all alone.

I hid under a tree in the forest. I was scared. I could not see the Cree, and I was afraid that they would find me. I didn't know which way to run."

"It started to rain," continued Running Wolf. "Then, I heard a bird calling at me. CAW! CAW! It was a crow calling from high in a tree. I saw the bushes move beneath the tree. The crow was telling me that my enemy was moving through those bushes. But the Cree were too close for me to run away, so I decided to follow the bird.

I climbed way up high into a tree and I hid behind some branches until my enemy walked away in the rain."

Running Wolf looked at Good Eagle and Little Leaf. Then he put his hand on their twin daughter. "Your name shall be 'Crow Calling,' " he said. Then he touched the baby boy. "And your name shall be 'Way Up High.' "

Good Eagle lifted his children up into the air and said, "Crow Calling and Way Up High! May you both live to honor the man who gave you these names."

Chapter 3

Buffalo Days

Chapter 3   After the Buffalo Jump
A Story of the Blackfoot Nation

Good Eagle and Little Leaf's children grew up quickly. They spent their days playing and learning the ways of the Blackfoot people. Crow Calling helped her mother and the other Blackfoot women to gather food. Way Up High and Buffalo Tail learned about hunting and fishing from their fathers and the other Blackfoot men.

Way Up High and Buffalo Tail became best friends. They played hunting and fighting games. They went swimming together in the river.

The boys learned how to ride horses together. They had contests to see who could throw a spear the farthest and they practiced shooting with bows and arrows.

One day in autumn, Way Up High and Buffalo Tail caught a young hawk. "Let's make a cage and keep it," said Way Up High. The boys killed rabbits and gophers and fed them to the hawk. All winter, they collected the feathers that dropped from the hawk's tail. In the spring, they put the feathers on their arrows. Then they opened the cage and let the hawk go free.

Chapter 3 After the Buffalo Jump

A Story of the Blackfoot Nation

Crow Calling and the other Blackfoot girls watched their mothers take the teepees down whenever the camp moved. And the girls helped to put the teepees back up again in the new camp. Each teepee had 19 wooden poles that were about 22 feet long. After the women put up the poles, they covered them with buffalo hides. The girls had the job of putting stones on the hides around the bottom of the teepee to hold the hides down on the ground.

Crow Calling watched her mother make robes out of buffalo hides. She watched the grandmothers collect roots and grasses. She watched them weave the roots and grasses into baskets.

Sometimes the women used wooden poles and buffalo hides to make a kind of sled called a *travois.* When it was time to move the camp, the women would load their supplies into the travois, and then tie the travois to a horse so that the horse could pull it to the next campsite.

Chapter 3   After the Buffalo Jump   **33**
               A Story of the Blackfoot Nation

When the tribe moved to a new campsite, even the dogs helped to carry loads.

Each of the girls learned to make a small travois. They would fill it with a few things, and then tie it to a dog. When the tribe moved to a new campsite, even the dogs helped to carry loads.

One day, Crow Calling watched her brother and Buffalo Tail play a hunting game by the river. The boys made a little buffalo out of mud. Then they pretended that they were on a buffalo hunt. They shot arrows at the pile of mud.

As Crow Calling watched the boys, she made some paint out of purple berries. Then she painted pictures of animals on three green leaves from a cottonwood tree. When she was finished, she told each boy to pick up a leaf and set it in the water. The three leaves stayed together as they floated down the river.

"That is a good sign," said Crow Calling.

"A good sign?" asked Buffalo Tail.

"Yes," said Crow Calling, "it is a sign that we will always be together.

Chapter 4

The Buffalo Jump

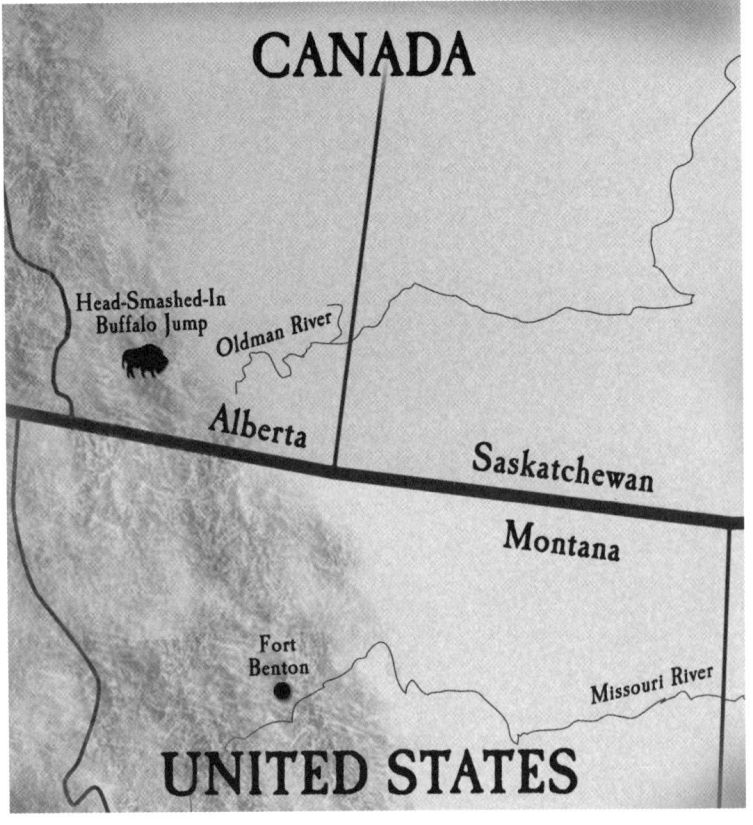

Chapter 4: After the Buffalo Jump
A Story of the Blackfoot Nation

When Crow Calling and Way Up High were 11 years old, they took part in their first buffalo jump.

It was in the middle of summer. Some of the grandfathers had set up a large teepee so that they could perform the Iniskim Ceremony. In this ceremony, they used a special rock called the Iniskim or Buffalo Rock. They believed that the rock would bring the buffalo from far away.

The next morning, Good Eagle and Running Wolf returned to camp with some news.

"We must move the camp to Head-Smashed-In," said Running Wolf. "The buffalo are moving in that direction."

Head-Smashed-In was the name of a Blackfoot camp near the bottom of a tall, rocky cliff. If the Blackfoot people were lucky, the warriors would frighten the buffalo into a stampede.

Then the warriors would keep the stampeding buffalo together until the buffalo ran off the cliff. The buffalo would fall more than 100 feet to their deaths on the rocks below.

Way Up High felt his heart pounding. He remembered what had happened the last time. At the last moment, the herd of buffalo had turned away from the cliff, and the tribe had lost their only chance in three years for a buffalo jump. Maybe this year would be different.

40 A Step into History

If the jump was successful, Crow Calling would help the Blackfoot women cut the hides, the meat and the bones from the dead buffalo. The tribe would have plenty of food and clothing for winter.

Before the stampede began, the tribe built a *drive lane* for the buffalo. The drive lane was like a big, wide street with sticks and piles of rocks on both sides. As the lane got closer to the cliff, it became narrower. When the herd ran toward the cliff, the buffalo in back would push against the buffalo in front and force them off the cliff.

"The buffalo have bad eyesight," explained Good Eagle to his son. "They think that our sticks and rocks are trees and walls, so they usually stay inside the drive lane and run off the cliff."

The drive lane was nearly ten miles long. There would have to be warriors all along the lane.

While the women were setting up camp near the cliff at Head-Smashed-In, the warriors began to move the buffalo slowly toward the drive lane.

Chapter 4 — After the Buffalo Jump
A Story of the Blackfoot Nation

Good Eagle dressed his son in a buffalo robe.

"I am proud of you, my son," he said. "Today you will be a buffalo runner like the other warriors."

"What will I do, father?" asked Way Up High.

"You will get on your hands and knees near the drive lane. You will make noises like a baby buffalo calling for its mother," his father told him. "Running Wolf and some other warriors will be on the other side of the herd.

They will each be wearing a wolf skin. They will crawl toward the herd and move the buffalo toward you and the drive lane," said Good Eagle.

"What if the buffalo stampede and run over me?" asked Way Up High.

Good Eagle laughed. "Then Way Up High will be Way Down Low," he said. Good Eagle knew that his son was afraid. "I still remember my first buffalo jump," said Good Eagle. "I know you'll do just fine, my son."

Chapter 4   After the Buffalo Jump   **45**
A Story of the Blackfoot Nation

Good Eagle took Way Up High on horseback out to the prairie, near to where the buffalo were grazing. Then Good Eagle led Buffalo Tail and a group of other warriors to some piles of rocks near the drive lane. They hid behind the piles of rocks. They would wait there for the buffalo to pass. Then they would jump out from behind the rocks and scare the buffalo to keep them in the drive lane.

Running Wolf and the other buffalo-runners put on their wolf-skins and began to crawl slowly across the prairie like wolves.

The buffalo began to walk toward Way Up High and the drive lanes.

Way Up High watched a buffalo and her baby come toward him. He could not believe how big the mother was. She was as tall as a full-grown man and weighed as much as six men! Way Up High moved away from her and crawled into the drive lane. He could see that the herd was following him.

When the herd was completely in the drive lane, Way Up High moved quickly to where his father was hiding.

A Step into History

Glenbow Archives, Calgary, Canada (NA-1497-37)

Chapter 4 — After the Buffalo Jump
A Story of the Blackfoot Nation

After all of the buffalo had passed by them, Good Eagle, Buffalo Tail, and the other warriors rode their horses out from behind the rocks. This scared the buffalo and they started to stampede in a cloud of dust.

Running Wolf ran up behind the herd waving his arms. "Go!" he yelled at a huge buffalo bull. The angry bull turned around, put his head down, and charged at Running Wolf. The bull hit Running Wolf with its horns and threw him to the ground. Running Wolf was bleeding badly.

Chapter 5

Preparing for Winter

Crow Calling and the other Blackfoot women below the cliff could hear the buffalo herd coming. The sound of the stampeding buffalo was as loud as thunder. Crow Calling could feel the earth shake as the buffalo pounded the ground with their hooves.

Crow Calling was amazed to see the large piles of buffalo bones at the bottom of the cliff. Her people had been coming to this place for more than 5,000 years.

Crow Calling remembered the story that her father had told her about a boy named Head-Smashed-In. He had climbed the rocks to watch the buffalo as they fell from the cliff. One of the buffalo had hit him, smashing into his head. The boy had fallen to his death with the buffalo.

Crow Calling saw a cloud of dust roll over the top of the cliff. This meant that the buffalo were getting closer. Then she saw the first buffalo at the front of the herd.

The buffalo tried to stop as they reached the edge of the cliff, but the other buffalo ran into them from behind, and pushed them over the edge.

Hundreds of buffalo began to fall like a dark waterfall over the cliff. Most of them died when they hit the rocks below. Warriors were waiting with spears to kill any buffalo that were still alive after the fall. The Blackfoot believed that if a buffalo got away, it would warn the other buffalo on the plains. If that happened, the buffalo jump would never be successful again.

Chapter 5 — After the Buffalo Jump
A Story of the Blackfoot Nation

All day long, the women were busy cutting up buffalo meat and cleaning hides. They would use every part of the buffalo, even some of the bones.

The women stacked the meat in big piles. They would boil some of it, roast some, and dry some in the sun. The dried meat would last all winter. Later, Crow Calling and her friends would pound some of the dried meat with a stone, and mix it with dried berries to make small cakes called *pemmican.*

Some women were scraping the buffalo hides. The hides would become covers for the teepees, blankets, shoes, clothes, rope, and bags for carrying medicine and supplies.

Other women cleaned the horns and bones. They would use the horns to make cups and spoons. They would use the bones to make arrowheads, knives, and jewelry. They would even use the buffalo's hooves to make glue.

Everyone was busy. It would take them several days to finish the work.

That night, the tribe would have a celebration because they knew there would be plenty of food for the winter.

Way Up High returned later from the hunt. He had found Running Wolf lying on the ground, bleeding badly. Way Up High could not wake Running Wolf up, so he called other men to help. They brought Running Wolf back to his teepee to watch over him.

A medicine woman named Old Owl Woman came to Running Wolf's teepee to see him.

The medicine woman was a kind of doctor. But she was also a holy leader who prayed to the Earth-Maker for help.

Old Owl Woman wrapped Running Wolf's cut with some medicine that she had made from plants. Then she prayed for him. But after three days, Running Wolf had still not spoken or opened his eyes. Old Owl Woman did not know if he would live.

Good Eagle came to see Old Owl Woman. He told her that he would dance for his friend in the Sun Dance.

"Yes, that will help him," Old Owl Woman told him. "You are a good friend."

Chapter 6

The Sun Dance

Many Blackfoot camps came together for the Sun Dance. At the Sun Dance, they would pray to the Earth-Maker for good weather and good health. "It is a time to give thanks for having enough food for the winter," Good Eagle told his children. "And it is a time for the people from different camps to talk and play games. I will be praying for Running Wolf at the Sun Dance," he said.

Each year, a different woman called the entire tribe together for the Sun Dance.

This year, Old Owl Woman led the dance. For four days, she fasted inside a special teepee. On the fifth day, she painted her face and then put on a special dress that was made from the skin of an elk.

Meanwhile, the men built a Sun Dance lodge. It was made out of poles and tree branches. The men also built a special table called an *altar* and put a buffalo skull on it. They carved pictures of animals into the wood. Then everyone in the tribe waited inside the lodge for Old Owl Woman.

At last, Old Owl Woman came into the lodge. One by one, the people came up to her. Old Owl Woman painted each person's face as a kind of blessing. Then, she gave everyone a piece of dried buffalo tongue. Each person turned toward the sun and said a prayer to the Earth-Maker. Then they ate the dried buffalo tongue.

Next, it was time for Good Eagle's dance. Good Eagle and the warriors had put up a tall pole in the middle of the lodge. The pole went through a hole at the top of the lodge.

First, Good Eagle's body was painted white. Then black dots and moons were painted on his white face and body. Some leaves from a sagebrush plant were tied around his head and arms and ankles.

An old warrior stepped up to Good Eagle. The warrior had two small, sharp sticks that were shaped like long needles. Good Eagle knew that one stick would be pushed into the flesh on his chest and the other would be pushed into the flesh on his back.

The old warrior held some of the flesh on Good Eagle's chest between his thumb and finger. Then the warrior pushed one of the sticks into Good Eagle's flesh. Good Eagle felt a sharp pain. The old warrior kept pushing the top of the stick through the flesh until the point of the stick came out again. When the old warrior finished, he turned Good Eagle around and pushed another stick through the flesh on his back.

Good Eagle could feel the blood dripping down his chest and down his back.

Next the old warrior tied one end of a rope to each stick. He tied the other end of each rope high up on the pole in the middle of the lodge.

Crow Calling cried as she watched her father dance around the pole. She knew what was going to happen next. She prayed for Running Wolf, but she also prayed for her father.

Good Eagle began to move away from the pole until the ropes pulled at the sticks. Then he leaned back until the sticks tore out of his flesh.

Chapter 6   After the Buffalo Jump
A Story of the Blackfoot Nation

The pain was terrible, but Good Eagle did not cry.

The old warrior said to him, "Now pray for your friend."

Good Eagle ran to the pole and prayed for Running Wolf to get well. The Sun Dance was over.

In a few days, Running Wolf woke up from his sleep. Each day, he became stronger.

But that winter, Old Owl Woman became weaker. Soon she was dying.

Everyone gathered around Old Owl Woman, and she told them about a dream that she had in her sleep.

"Beware of the blue-eyed wolf," she said. "He will come and show you things that you have never seen before. And you will think that he has magic. But the wolf will want you to live in wooden boxes, and he will give you tools that are made from iron," she said.

After saying these words, Old Owl Woman died. The people did not understand her words, but they did not forget them.

Chapter 7

The White People Come

NARA - Rocky Mountain Region - Record Group 75 - Records of the Bureau of Indian Affairs Blackfeet Agency, Industrial Survey

Chapter 7 After the Buffalo Jump
A Story of the Blackfoot Nation

Most of the Blackfoot did not realize that they had already met the blue-eyed wolf that Old Owl Woman had dreamed about. For many years, the Blackfoot had seen strange new people in their land. The skin of the new people was not as dark as the skin of the Blackfoot people, and some of these new people had blue eyes and yellow hair.

The new people told the Blackfoot that they had come from the east and the south. The people from the south called themselves Americans, and the people from the east called themselves Canadians.

But the Blackfoot called all of these new people *Napikwan.* In the Blackfoot language, this name means "Old Man's People." The Blackfoot believed that the whites came from so far away that Old Man must have made them.

At first, the white people had brought some good things. Before the whites arrived, the Blackfoot did not have any horses. Horses had changed the way that all Indian tribes lived. Before the Blackfoot had horses, they had used dogs to pull their travois whenever they moved their supplies from one camp to another.

Chapter 7 After the Buffalo Jump
A Story of the Blackfoot Nation

Now the Blackfoot used strong horses to pull the heavy travois.

The Blackfoot had hunted buffalo on foot. Now they could hunt on horseback. The Blackfoot had walked from place to place. Now, on horseback, they could travel much farther.

One day, Way Up High and his father rode their horses to Fort Benton to trade with the whites. Way Up High and Good Eagle had brought 60 buffalo robes to trade. From Canada, they rode south and crossed the border into the United States.

The Blackfoot called this border the *medicine line.*

When Good Eagle and Way Up High arrived at Fort Benton, they saw many other Indians who had also come there to trade with the whites. The Indians stood in a long line to trade their buffalo robes, blankets, and beads for guns, tools, tobacco, and whiskey.

The trading post was a busy place. "I like all of the things that we can get from the whites," Way Up High said to his father.

Chapter 7   After the Buffalo Jump
A Story of the Blackfoot Nation

75

"Yes," replied Good Eagle, "but these things have brought problems as well."

"What do you mean?" asked Way Up High.

"Their horses and guns have made our lives better," Good Eagle answered. "But the white man has also given us whiskey and a new kind of sickness. This sickness has killed some of our people. And the whiskey has made our warriors behave badly. They get drunk, and then they want to fight and kill each other," Good Eagle explained.

"Do you see all of the buffalo robes that these men have brought here to trade?" Good Eagle asked his son. "Our people have always used every part of the buffalo that we killed. Now many warriors are just cutting off the hide and leaving the meat to rot in the sun. It is not good to waste that meat," said Good Eagle. "It is becoming harder and harder to find the buffalo herd. Some people say that soon the buffalo will be gone."

Good Eagle traded 20 buffalo robes for a gun and then gave the gun to Way Up High. Then he traded more robes for bullets and tools that were made out of iron.

As Way Up High rode back home, he looked forward to hunting buffalo with his new gun. He was happy that his father had bought it for him. But he also thought about the 20 dead buffalo. He wished that he had made better use of their meat and bones.

A few weeks after the trip to Fort Benton, Good Eagle and Little Leaf both caught a sickness called smallpox. It was a new sickness that the white man had brought, and the Blackfoot medicine doctors did not have any way to cure it. Good Eagle and Little Leaf both died.

Chapter 8
Lame Bull's Treaty

Chapter 8: After the Buffalo Jump
A Story of the Blackfoot Nation

It was now 1855, and things were changing quickly. Every year, there were more and more whites coming to the plains to farm the land where the Blackfoot lived. The whites wanted to build houses and towns. They wanted to build roads and railroads. They were always fighting with the Blackfoot over the land. The whites raised cattle, so they did not care about the buffalo. The whites liked to shoot buffalo for fun.

There were still three tribes in the Blackfoot Nation: the North Blackfoot, the Bloods, and the Peigan.

Together these three tribes were the largest and strongest nation on the Great Plains. Most of the other Indian tribes were afraid of them, and the whites were afraid of them, also. So the whites decided to make a treaty with the Blackfoot.

The whites planned to meet with the Blackfoot leaders on the banks of the Missouri River, near Fort Benton. Running Wolf was now the chief of his camp, and he asked some of the other warriors to go with him.

Way Up High was only 12 years old, but Running Wolf wanted him to go because Way Up High was now the head of his family.

At the meeting, all of the Blackfoot chiefs sat and listened to the leader of the whites. His name was Governor Stevens.

"This country is your home," said Governor Stevens. "It will remain your home. But the buffalo will not last forever. We want to buy some of your land for our people.

We want you to live on farms to raise cattle and grow crops like we do," Governor Stevens told them. "We want you to live in peace with the other Indian tribes."

The chiefs listened as Governor Stevens spoke to them some more. "We want you to think of the white man as your Great Father. We want you and the Blackfoot children to learn English. We will help you build schools and houses. Where do you want your new homes to be?" the Governor asked them.

Some of the chiefs did not really understand what Governor Stevens was saying so they began to argue among themselves. They could not agree on what to do. Some of the chiefs did not trust the white man. They did not think that anyone could sell the land. The land was a gift from Old Man. People could use the land, but they could not own it.

At last, Chief Lame Bull spoke. "We will do what the white chiefs ask," he said. "The white chiefs want to do many things for us.

Let us listen to them," continued Chief Lame Bull. "I hope that the other Indian tribes will keep the peace that we will agree to here."

Back at the camp, Buffalo Tail was protecting the horses. Late one night, he heard a noise in the woods. He looked around and saw about 20 Cree warriors. They were coming to steal the horses!

Suddenly, the Cree started shooting to chase the horses away. Then, the Cree set fire to some of the teepees.

People woke up and ran outside. They tried to fight back, but they could not stop the Cree. Smoke filled the air and guns were exploding all around. People were screaming and the horses were running away into the night.

Buffalo Tail turned around and found himself face to face with a huge Cree warrior. The Cree knocked Buffalo Tail to the ground with his gun. Then the Cree jumped on top of Buffalo Tail and held him down by kneeling on him. The Cree lifted his ax into the air and smiled at Buffalo Tail.

The Cree knocked Buffalo Tail to the ground with his gun.

Chapter 8: After the Buffalo Jump
A Story of the Blackfoot Nation

As the ax started to come down, Buffalo Tail saw the Cree's eyes suddenly grow big. Then the warrior fell on top of Buffalo Tail. He had an arrow sticking out of his back.

Buffalo Tail looked up and saw Crow Calling with a bow in her hand. She helped Buffalo Tail to get up.

"Are you all right?" she asked.

"I think so," Buffalo Tail answered. "Thanks. You saved my life."

"I guess that means that you belong to me now," said Crow Calling.

Chapter 9
Death in Montana

Chapter 9 — After the Buffalo Jump
A Story of the Blackfoot Nation

In the summer of 1869, Running Wolf led his camp south across the medicine line into the state of Montana. They were looking for buffalo.

This was a bad time between the Blackfoot and the whites. The Blackfoot were angry about the treaty that Chief Lame Bull had made with the whites. Many more whites were coming to live on the plains. More and more Blackfoot were dying from smallpox. Others were having problems with whiskey. The rest of the tribe was worrying about food.

Would Running Wolf and his camp find any buffalo before the winter? What would happen to their old way of life?

In September, Running Wolf's camp met up with another group of Blackfoot who were led by a chief named Heavy Runner. Together, they had found a small herd of buffalo. But there would be barely enough buffalo meat for everyone to share.

In October, the weather started to turn cold.

It was too late in the year to go back up north to Canada, so Running Wolf and Heavy Runner decided to join together into one camp and stay in Montana until the spring.

Back on the plains in Canada, the Blackfoot people were hungry and angry. Some warriors began stealing and killing the white man's cattle for food. Other warriors even killed a few of the white settlers.

The angry whites took revenge and killed some Blackfoot people who had not done anything wrong.

On August 17, a group of 25 Blackfoot killed a white man named Malcolm Clark, even though he had married a Blackfoot woman and lived among the Blackfoot for more than 25 years.

The white settlers were scared but they came to the Blackfoot chiefs and said, "Give us the men who have killed Malcolm Clark." The Blackfoot chiefs knew that the warriors were from the camp of a leader named Mountain Chief. The chiefs said that they would find the warriors and turn them over to the whites, but it never happened.

By the beginning of 1870, the whites had grown tired of waiting.

It was now the middle of winter, and it was freezing cold. The wind howled across the Great Plains. One night, when the Blackfoot were huddled around their campfires, the U.S. Army attacked them. The soldiers thought they had found Mountain Chief's camp, so they started shooting at everyone. They wanted to kill the 25 warriors who had killed Malcolm Clark. But the soldiers had found the camp of Heavy Runner and Running Wolf.

Heavy Runner ran toward the soldiers. "Stop!" he yelled. "Why are you attacking us?" he asked. The soldiers answered Heavy Runner with gunshots before he could tell them who he was.

"Run!" called Running Wolf to his people. They all started to run. But Running Wolf was shot in the back before he could reach the woods.

The soldiers were afraid to go into the woods because they did not know where the Blackfoot were hiding. The soldiers did not know that the Blackfoot warriors had used up all of their bullets and arrows.

Way Up High, Crow Calling, and Buffalo Tail hid in the woods with some of the people from their camp. They could still hear the shooting and people screaming in the campsite. They saw smoke rise up into the sky. The soldiers had set the teepees on fire.

Then, everything became quiet. Way Up High, Crow Calling, and Buffalo Tail looked at each other. They were all scared. Way Up High spoke. "I don't want to fight anymore," he said. He stood up and walked out of the woods before anyone could stop him.

Way Up High walked out into the meadow. He did not see any soldiers. The black smoke from the burning camp went straight up into the blue sky before it was blown away by the wind. Way Up High heard a whistling sound. It was a bullet flying through the air.

Buffalo Tail and Crow Calling saw Way Up High fall to the ground. He was dead. Then they heard horses and footsteps in the woods. They thought the soldiers were coming to kill them.

Chapter 10

Treaty Number 7

Chapter 10: After the Buffalo Jump
A Story of the Blackfoot Nation

The Army soldiers killed almost 200 Blackfoot Indians in their attack on the camp. Crow Calling and Buffalo Tail were captured and sent to a reservation in Canada.

In 1877, the Blackfoot Nation and the Canadian government signed one last treaty. It was called Treaty Number 7. In this treaty, the Blackfoot nation gave up all of its land and agreed to be ruled by the Canadian government. The Blackfoot were moved onto a reservation.

Life on the reservation was not easy. The Blackfoot did not want to become farmers. They did not want to stop hunting buffalo and start eating cattle. At first, the government did not provide enough cattle or crops to feed the Blackfoot. Many people starved to death.

It was hard for the Blackfoot to give up their old way of life. Many of the younger Blackfoot were angry. They tried to steal horses from the whites. They continued to fight against their old Indian enemies.

Many of the older people could not get used to life on the reservation.

But after a while, most of the Blackfoot people did get used to living on the reservation. They tried to grow crops and raise cattle even though the land was poor for farming. They moved out of their teepees and started living in wooden houses. Their children began to go to school. They learned to speak English and French. Some Blackfoot even started following the white man's religion.

Buffalo Tail and Crow Calling got married and had a son. They wanted to give him a name that would remind them of the time when they were living free out on the Great Plains. They named their son "Tomorrow the Green Grass."

In the evenings, Crow Calling and Buffalo Tail would sit in front of their house with Tomorrow the Green Grass and watch the sun set slowly behind the hills.

Chapter 10 After the Buffalo Jump
A Story of the Blackfoot Nation

Buffalo Tail would look out at the fields and remember how he and Way Up High had learned to ride horses when they were boys. He missed seeing the buffalo running across the plains. He wished that he could go on one more buffalo hunt.

Crow Calling would sing a song that she had learned from her mother. As she sang, she thought about her son. She knew that he would never follow the buffalo, and the thought filled her with a great sadness.

The End

Bibliography

Selected Sources

Dempsey, Hugh A. *Indians of the Rocky Mountain Parks.* Calgary, Alberta, Canada: Fifth House Ltd, 1998.

Ewers, John. C. *The Blackfeet: Raiders on the Northwestern Plains.* Norman, Oklahoma: University of Oklahoma Press, 1958.

Mountain Horse, Mike. *My People the Bloods.* Ed. and introduction by Hugh A. Dempsey. Calgary, Alberta, Canada: Glenbow Museum, 1979.

Swanson, Diane. *Buffalo Sunrise: The Story of a North American Giant.* Vancouver, British Columbia, Canada: Whitecap Books, 1996.

Ward, Donald. *The People: A Historical Guide to the First Nations of Alberta, Saskatchewan, and Manitoba.* Calgary, Alberta, Canada: Fifth House Ltd, 1995.

Interviews:

Shirley Bruised Head. Interview with author at Head-Smashed-In Buffalo Jump Interpretive Centre. Alberta, Canada, 1999.

Websites:

Head-Smashed-In Buffalo Jump. UNESCO World Heritage Site. Alberta, Canada. www.head-smashed-in.com

A Note from the Start-to-Finish™ Editors

This book has been divided into approximately equal short chapters so that the student can read a chapter and take the cloze test in one reading session. This length constraint has sometimes required the authors and editors to make transitions in mid-chapter or to break up chapters in unexpected places.

You will also notice that Start-to-Finish™ Books look different from other high-low readers and chapter books. The text layout of this book coordinates with the other media components (CD and audiocassette) of the Start-to-Finish™ series.

The text in the book matches, line for line and page for page, the text shown on the computer screen, enabling readers to follow along easily in the book. Each page ends in a complete sentence so that the student can either practice the page (repeat reading) or turn the page to continue with the story. If the next sentence cannot fit on the page in its entirety, it has been shifted to the next page. For this reason, the sentence at the top of a page may not be indented, signaling that it is part of the paragraph from the preceding page.

Words are not hyphenated at the ends of lines. This sometimes creates extra space at the end of a line, but eliminates confusion for the struggling reader.